The Rat-Catcher's Son

**and
other stories**

by
CAROLYN LONDON

Illustrations by Vincenzo D'Amico

SONLIGHT
The way you wish you'd been taught.

SIM

**The Rat-Catcher's Son
And Other Stories**

By SIM International

Printed in the United States of America

First Sonlight Curriculum, Ltd. Edition, 2003

For a catalog of Sonlight Curriculum materials
For the home school, write:

SONLIGHT CURRICULUM, LTD
8042 South Grant Way
Littleton, CO 80122-2705
USA

Or email: main@sonlight.com

Contents

1

Angel of Light

"Baba," I begged, "tell us a story."

"A story? You lazy children! Look, the sky isn't even dark and you're back from the farm. And now you want me to tell you a story."

The old man's gruff voice didn't frighten us in the least.

"See," I said, pointing to the red ball hanging in the dusty desert sky, "the sun is red. And look, Baba, see the basket of roasted peanuts we've brought you."

"Trying to bribe me, huh?" Grandfather's eyes twinkled as he reached into the basket for a handful of nuts. "All right, put another piece of wood on the fire and stir that pot of porridge."

"Why are you cooking the porridge? Where's Mother?" I asked as I lifted the cover off the cooking pot. *Ayah!* That porridge smelled good.

"Your father and mother have gone to the village of Crocodile Lake to talk to the people of the Lord Jesus. Hurry now, stir the porridge and then put your lazy bones down on the mat and I'll tell you a story the old people used to tell me when I was a boy."

My young brother, Little Lion, put another stick of wood in the fire, and I stirred the porridge. After all, a girl's job is cooking, so I was sure I could stir it better than Little Lion could. All African girls are good cooks.

Then I ran into the house and pulled out the sleeping mat Grandfather had made from the skin of a lion. It was a fine mat and I was proud that my grandfather had been such a brave hunter.

"Now, tell us the story," we begged as we made ourselves comfortable on the lion skin.

The fire cast a red glow on the old man's dark face. It wouldn't be long before the sun was completely swallowed up by the earth. Already the wind from the desert had a chill in it.

Baba pulled at his scrawny gray beard. I knew the signs. First he'd tug at his beard, then he'd poke at the fire, and then he'd settle back, just like he was doing now, and we'd hear a good story.

"Once upon a time, a long, long time ago—"

Oh, how I love stories that begin "Once upon a time." I grabbed a mouthful of peanuts and huddled up closer to the fire.

"A long time ago there was a farmer named Audu. Now, Audu was very pleased with himself. His crops were doing well, the rains were just right, and he was sure he was going to make a lot of money farming that season.

"One night Audu came home to his wife. He was all puffed up with pleasure. 'Yes, wife,' he boasted, 'we're going to have a lot of money this year. *Ayah!* Everything's going well with me. *Haba!* My farm is better than any of my neighbors. And do you know what? I'm sure that God is going to be very pleased with me. Do you know what I did today? I gave a penny—a whole penny—to a beggar!'

" 'A *penny!*' his wife screeched at him. 'Why did you waste money? By the beard of the sacred goat! A penny! I could have bought a new bead for my necklace with that money. And you go and give it to a worthless beggar.'

" '*Ayah!*' Audu groaned, 'I really didn't want

to give it to him, but you see, I've been thinking—'

" 'Since when?'

"Audu ignored his wife and went on speaking. 'I think we ought to buy some favor with
God. After all, maybe if I give a few pennies to
beggars, I'll get a good reward from God. Yes, a
penny should buy some kind of a reward in
heaven.'

" 'Ha! What makes you so sure you're even
going to get to heaven?' his wife snorted in disgust.

" *'Ayah!* I gave him a penny, and why, of
course, I'm going to heaven—' Audu's voice
trailed off and he said softly, 'I hope—I hope
I'm going to heaven.' Then, more cheerfully
he said, 'Besides, once before I gave a penny to
a beggar. That's two pennies now; there ought
to be some reward.'

" 'Well, I know what will be a lot better reward right now,' his wife replied angrily.

" 'Yes? What?' Audu snapped.

" 'You should fix the roof. Look, the grass is
getting all ragged on the roof, and the rafters
are weak.'

" 'Fix the roof! Fix the roof! Fix the roof!

Woman, when will you quit nagging at me? Don't you know I've got a lot more important things to be doing besides fixing the roof? Can't you forget the roof?'

" 'Oh,' his wife said, and shrugged, 'I can forget the roof, but I don't think you'll be able to forget your new robe that the rain ruined last night.'

" 'What happened to my new robe?'

" 'The roof leaked because you didn't fix it, and the rain made a big stain on your nice new robe.'

" 'My new robe ruined? *Haba,* woman! Why didn't you put it where it couldn't be rained on? You are a lazy, careless woman, letting my new robe be ruined.'

" 'If you'd fix the roof it wouldn't have gotten rained on.'

" 'Now it's my fault because you were so lazy.'

"And so the fight went on," Baba told us. "And the roof didn't get fixed. But one day Audu came home from his farm with a big smile on his face.

" 'Well, Wife, it's all right about that robe. I'm going to get a big reward in heaven. You know I couldn't get the stain out, and it looked just terrible. So today I gave it to a blind beggar. He won't know the difference. Ha! I told him it was a very fine robe. *Ayah!* Just think of all the reward I'll get. Two pennies and a fine new robe!' "

Baba stopped and reached for a peanut. "Better stir the porridge again."

I jumped up and took the stirring stick, and while I stirred the thick guinea-corn porridge I was thinking about the story.

"Baba, didn't Audu know he couldn't buy a reward in heaven?"

"No, poor Audu didn't know he couldn't buy favor with God. Even if he'd given a hundred pounds to the beggar, he couldn't buy any favor with God. And if he'd given a hundred robes, that wouldn't have bought him a robe of righteousness. No, the only thing that God wants is faith in the Lord Jesus Christ. But you see, Audu had never heard of the Lord Jesus."

I licked the porridge off the stirring stick and propped it up in the wooden mortar where Mother pounds the grain for our porridge. Then I settled back on the lion-skin mat.

"Now tell us the rest of the story," I prompted my grandfather.

"Well," Baba drawled as he tugged at his beard, "that night Audu went to sleep thinking how very good he was, and what a wonderful reward the Lord would give him because he was so good. In the middle of the night, when the whole town was asleep, a thief came crawling out of the darkness. The thief was looking for food. Growing up over the roof of Audu's house was a large pumpkin vine.

" 'Hmm, a nice juicy pumpkin,' the thief said, smacking his lips. *'Madalla!* I'll just crawl up that little old vine and get myself a nice fat pumpkin.'

" 'Softly now, quiet-like!' the thief told himself. 'Just a little closer—ah—now—*up!* Up the vine!' The thief put one hand over the other and crept up to the top of the roof. All of a sudden—*crash!*

"Audu woke up with a start. 'What happened? What's the matter? Who—what stepped on my face? *Wayyo!* What's this? The roof is open! Oh, my! What's this standing over my bed? Who—who—what are you?'

" 'I'm an angel—an angel of light,' the quick-thinking thief answered.

" 'An angel! How wonderful! Welcome, An-

The thief crept up to the top of the roof. All of a sudden — crash!

gel. I am very glad to see you. But, I do wish that you hadn't stepped on my head when you came in. But, never mind, I'm very glad to see you. Ah, yes, an angel, an angel of light. Not very light-footed, but an angel, nevertheless. Welcome! And did you record the good gift I gave the blind beggar today?'

" 'Aaah! Did you give a gift? Yes, I suppose I did record it. But, then, you see, I have so very many gifts to record that I can't keep track of them all,' the so-called angel replied.

" 'But—but,' Audu protested, 'surely you couldn't forget this gift! *Ayah!* I gave a beautiful satin robe to a blind beggar. A very fine robe, and new, and nice and clean and shiny.'

" '*Ap!*' Audu's wife grumbled sleepily. She pulled the blanket up over her ears and turned over. 'What are you mumbling about? Wake up! You must be dreaming. You were talking about a robe—a good robe. You know that it was an old robe. And it wasn't satin; it was cotton. Sh, I want to sleep.'

" 'Hush, wife! I'm talking to an angel!'

" 'An angel! How in the world did an angel get in here?'

" 'Through the roof. That's how he got in.

And right on my face he landed. Yes, I know
that God sent this angel to reward me.'

"But his wife hadn't heard a word he'd said;
she'd fallen fast asleep again.

" 'Ah, yes,' the thief said softly. 'And I think
you are a good man, and I wouldn't want to forget that robe. You wouldn't want me to forget
that robe you gave to the beggar, now would
you?'

" 'Of course I wouldn't want you to forget it.
I'm planning on that robe to be my reward in
heaven.'

" 'Ah, yes, heaven. Hmm, now let's see, if
you'd only do something to make me remember
that robe. Now let's see, if you gave me ten
pounds I'm sure I would remember.'

" 'Ten pounds! I haven't got that much money. I'll tell you the truth, I only have two
pounds. I will give you all my money to help
you remember my robe so that I will get a reward in heaven.'

" 'I'd remember better if you gave me seven
pounds.'

" 'I will give you five pounds,' Audu said.

" 'Good! Bring your money,' the thief or-
dered.

"I'm an angel — an angel of light," the quick-thinking thief answered.

"Audu raised the edge of his mat, reached into a small hole under it, and pulled out a bag of money. He counted out the shillings into the thief's hand. 'One, two, three, four—and five pounds,' Audu said happily. 'Now, for five pounds I have bought your memory. And you will write in the big book in heaven that I gave a fine robe to a beggar. You won't forget?'

" 'No, I won't forget,' the angel said as he put the money in his pocket. 'Now, if you'll just move your great big feet so I can get out of the door. Thank you.'

" 'Out the door? Aren't you going back to heaven through the roof?'

" 'No, I prefer to leave this way. Good-bye.'

"Audu rolled over on his sleeping mat. 'It's strange, I never heard of an angel using a door.'

" 'Audu!' his wife said angrily, 'You woke me up again.'

" 'Wife,' Audu said happily, 'I was talking to an angel.'

" 'An angel?' she shouted. 'How did an angel get in here?'

" 'Through the roof,' Audu answered. 'I gave him five pounds to be sure and remember me when he got back to heaven. Something's worrying me though.'

" '*Five pounds!* Husband, is your head divided? Are you crazy? Why didn't you give him only two?'

" 'He wouldn't remember for only two,' Audu said."

Baba stopped telling the story.

"Oh, Baba, don't stop there," I said. "I want to hear the rest of the story."

"You'll hear the rest. But now you'd better stir that porridge again. You don't want your mother and father to have to eat lumpy food, do you?"

Little Lion put another stick of wood on the fire while I stirred the evening meal.

"Baba," Little Lion asked, "why didn't Audu know that he couldn't get a reward in heaven by giving money? Humph! Didn't he know that only the Lord Jesus could take him to heaven?"

Baba looked very serious as we sat down beside him again. He tugged at his gray beard and said, "There are a lot of people, even today, who don't know how to get to heaven."

Little Lion said, "But *we* know how."

I was anxious to hear the rest of the story, but

Baba didn't seem to mind Little Lion interrupting. "That's because the missionaries came and told us about the Lord Jesus," he said.

"And that's why Father and Mother have gone to Crocodile Lake," Little Lion said as he slowly ate a peanut. "They've gone to tell the people there how to get to heaven, just like the missionaries told us. I wish someone had told Audu. Baba, what happened to Audu?"

"Well," Baba said, "Audu and his wife talked about the angel for a long time, and finally they drifted off to sleep. But very early in the morning, as soon as it was light, Audu jumped out of bed.

" 'Where are you going?' his wife asked.

" 'I'm going over to the neighbors, and I'm going to tell them about the wonderful thing that happened to us last night. Just think, it isn't everyone who has an angel visit them in the middle of the night. I knew that I was better than anyone else around here. And God sent an angel.'

"Audu's wife had gotten out of bed and had gone to the door while he was speaking. Suddenly she screamed, 'Audu! Look!' She pointed to the ground. 'Look at that big footprint! And look! There's another!'

"They ran out of the house and followed the footprints.

" 'By the beard of the sacred goat!' Audu's wife exclaimed. 'That angel had big feet.'

" 'That I know. Didn't he land right on my face when he came through the roof?'

" 'Hmm. And look at the hole in the roof!' his wife said. 'That's strange—'

" 'What's strange?' Audu asked crossly.

" 'Did you ever hear of an angel breaking the roof when he came to visit someone?'

" 'And *look!*' Audu said. 'Look at the size of his footprints! And he called *my* feet big.'

" 'Look, Audu!' his wife said, pointing to the roof. 'The pumpkin vine—it's been torn right off!'

"Audu examined the vine. He walked all around the outside of his house. Suddenly he called out in a shrill voice, 'Wife! Wife! The angel didn't come down from heaven. Here are his footprints leading to the house. He tried to climb the pumpkin vine, and he fell through the roof!'

" 'I told you to fix the roof!'

" 'I've been robbed! Thief! I've been robbed!
He stole my money. Five pounds! Help! I've
been robbed. That wasn't an angel! That was
a thief!' "

"Oh, Baba!" I said, rolling on the ground
with laughter. "What a silly man Audu was.
That really was a good story."

"And here come your father and mother,"
Baba said. "Now run meet them."

2

The Boastful Man

I stirred the gravy with the stirring stick.

"Baba, doesn't this fish gravy smell good?" I said. "Won't Father be proud of me when he comes back from the farm? Do you know what he'll say to me? He'll say, 'Sunday, my daughter, this is the very best fish gravy in the whole wide world.' That's what he'll say. Fish gravy! I just love fish gravy. It surely will taste good on this porridge."

Baba just smiled at me and went on braiding his rope. My grandfather can make the very strongest rope in the world. I licked the stirring stick and laid it down on the mat.

"Baba, teach me to make rope," I begged.

"Humph! Girls don't make ropes," Little Lion snorted at me. "Rope-making is for men!"

"Bet I could make a better rope than you can,

even if I am a girl," I told him. "I could braid
it strong and smooth-- And, anyway, I'm smarter
than you are, so I could make a better rope. So
there!"

Boys! Just 'cause they're boys, they think
girls can't do anything.

"Haba! You said fishing was for boys. And
look! Who caught the biggest fish? I did. And
all you caught was a little one not as long as
your own hand. I caught the biggest fish, and
I'm the smartest. And my fish gravy tastes better than anyone else's in the whole world! So
there!"

"Sunday, you'd better stir that porridge again.
It smells like it might be sticking." Grandfather
sounded a little bit cross.

"My porridge never sticks," I boasted. But
even so, just to be sure, I gave it a good stirring.
Well, it was stuck. But just a little bit, not very
much.

I watched Little Lion trying to make the rope
fibers lie down smooth.

"My, you're clumsy," I told him.

"Well, Sunday, you must remember Little
Lion's only six years old." Baba sounded crosser
than ever.

"Bet I could have done better when I was six." I pouted.

Grandfather ignored me and turned to my brother.

"Little Lion, did you get your prize today in school?" Grandfather asked.

"Sure did." Little Lion sounded happy. He dug down into the deep pocket of his shirt and said, "Look at this pretty card with the gold star on it."

Grandfather examined the card closely. "Hmm, very, very good."

"Ha!" I said, "It's only a little card. Who wants a little old card with a star?" I couldn't help it, but two big fat tears ran down my cheeks. "Anybody could win a card like that. I could, too, if I really wanted to. I'm smarter than Little Lion."

"I think that porridge is done now, Sunday," Baba said softly to me. "Put it to one side and come sit down here with me, and I'll tell you a story."

I just love to hear Baba's stories, and for a minute I was almost happy. Who wants a little old card, anyway?

Baba moved over to let me sit beside him on

the lion-skin mat. It isn't every girl who gets to sit on a special lion-skin mat. Why, my grandfather is the best hunter in the whole world.

"I'm going to tell you a story our people have known for many, many years," Grandfather began.

Baba took a stick and poked at the fire. The red flames made a rosy glow on his long white robe. He sighed, pulled at his beard, and then began.

"One time, a long, long time ago, there lived a farmer named Sule. One day Sule was coming home from his farm. He had a bundle of grain on his head. As he approached the edge of town, he met his friend Ali.

" 'Hello, Ali. See this wonderful bundle of grain I've got? Not many farmers around here can grow such nice grain as I can. Say, what's that in your basket? Fish? Let me see. Pretty nice fish, but I've seen a lot bigger ones. Yes, sir, I caught one last week that was twice as big as your biggest one. But you've done all right. 'Course, when you don't have any better net than the one you've got, you can't expect to catch big fish. Now, if you only had a good net like I've got— What's the matter, Ali, do you have to rush off? Well, good-bye.'

"Sule walked down the path toward his house. 'It's funny,' he said. 'Ali's never in a hurry when he talks to the other men about fishing—' Sule shifted his bundle of grain to a more comfortable position. 'Wonder why he was in such a hurry?'

"Just after Sule had entered the village, he met another man.

" 'Hello, Sani, I was wanting someone to talk to. Come on down to the house and have a drink of gruel with me. You know, my wife makes the best gruel and buttermilk in town. Nobody's got a smarter wife than I have. Yes, sir, my wife is the best cook in the whole town. What's the matter, you have to leave? So soon? Too bad.'

"Sule followed the little sandy path down to his house. 'Strange,' he said, 'wonder why Sani didn't want to come home with me?'

"Just as Sule got to his front gate he met another man coming in from the forest.

" 'Well, Bako, I see you've caught a leopard. You ought to get three pounds for that skin. 'Course, it isn't a very big leopard. You remember the one I killed last year? Now that was a fine big leopard. If the man at the trading post hadn't been so stupid, he would have known how good it was; he would have given me a lot of money. As it was, he only gave me two pounds ten. But it was much bigger than the one you've got there.

" 'Were you afraid when you trapped it? I imagine you were. I wasn't the least bit afraid. Why, even when I was a child, I was the bravest person in our whole village. I remember one time when my mother heard a noise outside our house. She thought it was a hyena and was afraid. But I looked out and saw it was only a dog, so I drove it away. Of course, it was a great big dog.

" 'Come on in and sit down for a while. I have a nice new stool I just carved. Good piece of workmanship, if I do say so myself. I just finished it. Oh, you have to go? Well, some other day, then.'

"Poor Sule. He went into his compound and sat down on his new stool.

" 'Wonder why no one ever comes in to visit me?' he said to himself."

"Oh, Baba," I laughed, "I know why. Wasn't

"You remember the one I killed last year? Now that was a fine big leopard."

he stupid? All that bragging. Of course, no one likes a person who brags all the time. Why—I—I—"

"Yes, Sunday, what were you saying?" Baba asked me.

"Oh, nothing. Let's hear some more of the story."

Grandfather smiled at me. Then he went on with his story. Somehow, I didn't feel too good.

"Well, one day Sule came home from town," Grandfather said. "Sule's wife was busy grinding grain. He walked over to her and started laughing.

" 'Wife,' he said, 'Jabo's over at the blacksmith's getting his tooth dug out. You ought to have heard him screaming. Why, do you remember, Ladi, when I had that toothache last year, and you thought I was going to die?'

" 'I didn't think you were going to *die*. I just said you groaned like you might die,' his wife answered.

" 'Yes, that's what I mean. I suffered so terribly. Well, I was just telling Jabo how brave I was last year when I had that bad toothache. I told him no one heard *me* screaming. Don't know why he didn't seem to appreciate how brave I was. He just told me to go away! Nobody really understands how much I suffered. I was so brave.'

"Ladi just ignored Sule and went on grinding her grain.

" 'Say,' Sule continued, 'did you know that the old blind grandmother down the street gave a whole shilling to a beggar? Wonder why she didn't tell me about it. I saw her just this afternoon. The old beggar told me. 'Course, a shilling isn't very much. I gave a whole bundle of grain to the teacher last harvest, or was it the harvest before? After all, a shilling isn't very much, not compared to a bundle of grain.

" 'And do you remember how I hired that drummer to sit out in front of the house and sing about my good gift? Didn't he sound good? It made my stomach all sweet and warm to hear him sing,

> In the town of Elephant Head
> When all's been done and said,
> Farmer Sule is the best
> Much more generous
> Than the rest.

" 'He really knew how to sing. But then, of

course, I live such a good life, and I'm so brave and kind and generous that it wouldn't be hard for him to make up a good song about me.' "

"Baba," Little Lion spoke up. "Do you think Farmer Sule ever heard the Bible verse we learned in Sunday school the other day—the one that says, 'Let nothing be done—be done—through strife or vainglory—vainglory—' Uh, I forget the rest."

"Stupid!" I told him. "The verse is easy. 'Let nothing be done through strife or vainglory; but in lowliness of mind let each esteem other better than themselves.' See, I know it."

I wondered why Baba looked at me so strangely when I finished saying the verse. He didn't say anything, though; he just went on with the story.

"Well, one day Sule's wife, Ladi, got tired of all Sule's boasting, so she went to her mother and asked if she couldn't help make Sule stop boasting.

" 'Yes, I think I have a plan that will work,' Ladi's mother said. 'When you get home, you tell Sule you want to visit your cousin who lives at the other side of the jungle. Tell him you are afraid to go by yourself. Ask him to walk

with you through the jungle to protect you.
Take your younger sister with you, and halfway
through the jungle I will have your brother
meet you. Brother will have a mask on and
Sule won't recognize him. Sule will think it is a
robber. We'll see how brave Sule is. Maybe he
will learn something about himself.'

"Early the next morning Sule, his wife, Ladi,
and her younger sister set out through the jungle. Sule was bragging as usual.

" 'Well, I'm certainly glad that I can go along
and protect you women. You're very fortunate
to have a big brave man like me along to take
care of you. Why, I'm not afraid of anything—
alive or dead. I'm the bravest— *Wayyo! Wayyo!*
W-what's t-this?'

"Sule screamed and fell to the ground as a
big burly man stepped out from behind a huge
mahogany tree.

" 'I am the chief of the robbers. I shall kill
you and take your gold,' Ladi's brother growled
at the frightened Sule and the two women who
were trying hard to hide their laughing. 'But
first, I shall ask your names. What is your name?'
The so-called robber turned to Ladi.

" 'Please, sir, don't kill me.' Ladi's voice

shook with laughter, but Sule, cowering in the mud of the jungle path, thought it was fear. 'Please, sir, my name is Ladi.'

" 'Ladi!' the make-believe robber cried. 'I would never kill anyone named Ladi. Ladi was my mother's name.'

"Then the robber turned to the younger sister. 'Tell me what your name is,' he demanded.

" 'Please, sir, please don't kill me,' she giggled. 'My name is Ladi.'

" 'You, too, may go free. I could never kill anyone named Ladi. But—' And the big man turned to Sule. '*You* shall die. I shall kill you.'

" 'Please, please, don't kill me.' Sule rolled in the mud in fear. 'Please, sir, don't kill me.'

" '*I shall kill you!*'

" 'Please, sir, please don't kill me. Please, sir, my name is Ladi.' Sule cried.

" '*Ladi!* Your name can't be Ladi. That's a woman's name!' the robber roared.

" 'Please, sir,' Sule said, trying to cover his big black beard. 'Please, sir, I am—I am a woman.'

"And at that Ladi and her sister and the so-called robber all began to laugh. They laughed

ease sir," Sule said trying to cover his big black beard, "I am a woman."

and they laughed. They laughed until they cried.

"Poor Sule couldn't imagine what was the matter until the brother took off the mask. Then Sule was so embarrassed that he went home and never bragged again."

"Oh, that was a funny story." Little Lion was doubled up with laughter.

But you know, somehow I didn't think it was so funny.

"Baba," I whispered softly, "I-I'll try not to be like Sule."

I looked over at Little Lion's card with the gold star.

"Little Lion, I think your card is beautiful. I'm going to try to study real hard, and maybe I can get one next month. I think you were smart to get one."

3

The Wild Water Buffalo

Baba found me crying.

"What's the matter, Sunday?"

"N-nothing," I lied.

Nothing wrong with me! Everything was wrong. Everything. But I knew an old man like my grandfather would never understand. How could he understand? He's so old. I wished he'd go away and leave me alone. I just wanted to cry and be miserable. But, there he was, standing above me.

Go away! I screamed at him in my heart. *I hate you. I hate everybody!* I wanted to shout this out loud at him, but I didn't dare. There're just some things you can't do—even to your dear old *baba*. He was a dear. I guess I really didn't hate him. I guess I don't really hate everybody —just Laraba—and Mari—and all the rest of the girls who are going to have a harvest feast in their classroom.

Baba smiled down at me. I wished he wouldn't smile. He took his small garden hoe from off his shoulder and walked past me. He wiggled the fence post until it stood straight, and then he stamped the ground down firmly. It wasn't our post; it belonged to the man next door.

"Don't know why you bother fixing that old post," I grumbled.

"Garba's been very busy on his farm," Baba told me. "It didn't do me any harm to help him out. And, well, I like doing little things like that. Don't you, Sunday?"

"Like what?" I muttered. The only thing I liked right now was lying out here in the shade by the fence. It's my very own private place. The fence makes a little bend, and it's just big enough for me to cuddle up in and to figure out my problems. Our big mango tree makes a nice wall on the other side, so it is a very private place.

I wished Baba would go away and leave me alone in my private place. I wanted to sit here and cry and— But he wasn't going away. He was standing there talking.

"Like helping people when they need help," he said.

Baba didn't look like he'd planned to go away very soon, either. He tossed his hoe down to one side and sat down on a big stone. He pulled a small bunch of leaves off the mango tree and swooshed the flies away.

I didn't answer him.

Baba reached into his long, deep pocket of his robe. Out came a small bundle of dried grass and a long needle. Now I knew he didn't intend to go away. Baba settled back comfortably and began making a *faifai* mat. Mother uses these little round mats to cover the tops of water jars so that the lizards and flies won't get in. Mother says Baba's mats are a big help to her.

I wished he'd stop making mats and go away and let me cry in peace. Laraba's been my best friend, and I'd just sent her away from here. Oh, we'd had a big fight! I didn't see why I had to help her!

"Want to hear a story, Sunday?"

I didn't, but what could I say?

I just sat quietly. Baba didn't wait for me to answer. He just started telling his story.

"One time, a long, long time ago, there was a woman who lived in Kano City. She was a very cross old woman. Every time she would see a small child crying, she would run out and scream at the child, 'Stop your crying, or I'll beat you!'

"The poor frightened child would run to his mother and tell her that the old woman was going to hurt him. Of course, the mother would then be very angry with the cross old woman.

"This old woman, whose name was Abu, never had a kind word for anyone. When the water carriers would come into her compound and fill her pots with water, she would scream at them and tell them they hadn't brought her a full measure. She would never help them with their loads or steady the pots for them when they took them off their heads. 'Why should I help them?' she would grumble. 'They are getting paid to bring water!'

"If one of her neighbors was going to have a naming-day feast and wanted to borrow some of Abu's cooking pots, Abu would grumble and fuss.

" 'Why should I loan you my cooking pots? You might break them. Why don't you buy some of your own?' Maybe Abu would loan the cooking pots, and maybe she wouldn't. But even if she did, the neighbor would feel so badly about the way Abu had fussed at her that she'd go away very unhappy.

"And then Abu would be unhappy. She didn't know what caused her unhappy feeling.

"If any of the neighbors was sick or in trouble, Abu would watch the other people going to help him out. But all Abu would do was to say, 'Well, it's all your own fault. You got yourself into this trouble; now don't expect me to get you out.' And she'd laugh at the people who helped those in trouble.

"Abu was very unhappy. And, as I say, she didn't know what caused her unhappy feeling. Every time she'd hear the neighbors laughing and visiting together at a naming-day feast—or she'd see the water carriers leaving the house across the path with a big smile on their faces— or she'd heard someone saying, 'Oh, thank you very much for helping me; I just don't know what I'd have done without you'—then her stomach would feel dirty.

Stomach feel dirty? Whose stomach could feel dirtier than mine felt? Do you suppose Baba had heard me fighting with Laraba? But, after all, Laraba had it coming to her. Why should I help clean up the schoolhouse? It isn't my class that's having the feast.

Baba continued, "And when Abu went to the market, everyone dreaded to see her come. The women would hastily pack up their loads and turn their backs on Abu. If she tried to buy anything they would say, 'Everything's sold, we are going home. Go try someone else and see if they have what you want.'

"Now, you can imagine poor Abu was very miserable. And, of course, her husband wasn't very happy either. He dreaded to come home at night because he knew that instead of a pleasant word and a good supper of porridge and gravy, Abu would scold him for being late. Or, she'd scold him for being early. Or, she'd scold him for not doing something. Or, she'd scold him for doing it.

"No, life was not very pleasant in Abu's compound. Abu was very lonely. Abu didn't really like not having friends," Baba said.

I've got friends, I thought. *Just 'cause I wouldn't help Laraba clean up the schoolhouse, and she said I couldn't come to the class feast— I've got lots of friends. Oh, dear, maybe I should have— Oh, who cares about Abu, anyway? But, well—*

Baba looked at me. I think he saw me trying to wipe away a tear that was tickling the side of my nose. I really felt bad about Laraba. Maybe I should have helped—

Baba went on with his story:

"One day Abu decided something had to be done about this way of living."

Baba stopped talking and took off his white cotton cap. It was a long cap, like all our old men wear, and it makes a very good extra pocket. I watched Grandfather as he pulled out a small leaf-wrapped bundle from his cap. He unwrapped the leaves and handed me a piece of *jire*. I love to chew this nice sweet pitch that comes from the gum arabic tree. But even the *jire* didn't taste so good today. Baba selected a piece for himself and carefully rewrapped the rest and tucked it into his cap. He popped the gum into his mouth and went on with his story.

"So one fine day Abu decided she'd go to the judge who was the wisest man in town and ask him what to do. The wise old judge knew Abu very well. Even he had received tongue lashings from Abu on many occasions. And so he was more than a little surprised when Abu came into his entrance hut and sat down very meekly and quietly on a mat before him.

" 'Long life to you, Judge,' Abu began her speech. 'I have come to ask you a favor. There is something I want very much and something I need very much. I think you are the wisest man in the town, and you may be able to give me the medicine I need. I want you to give me some medicine that will make people like me.

" 'My husband doesn't love me. My neighbors don't love me. Even the dogs tuck their tails between their legs and run howling down the street when I come out of my gate.'

" 'Hmm.' The wise old judge was surprised at this request. 'Hmm. So you want medicine to make people like you?'

" 'Yes, sir, and I know you are very wise and can help me,' Abu answered.

" 'Hmm. Well, I think you have already begun to find this medicine.' The wise old judge smiled.

" 'Please, sir, I don't understand. Please, please give me this medicine!' Abu begged.

" 'I can give you this medicine,' the judge

promised. 'But it is a very difficult medicine. It is very hard to obtain.'

" 'I do not care how hard it is,' Abu cried. 'I want that medicine. I will do anything. I will pay anything. Just give me the medicine.'

" 'All right,' the judge promised. 'I will give you the medicine. But first you must go out into the bush and bring me a gourd full of milk from a wild buffalo.'

" 'A wild buffalo!' Abu cried out in amazement. 'Oh, that would be impossible. How would I ever get near a wild buffalo? Isn't there a simpler way to get this medicine? I would never get near a wild buffalo.'

" 'No,' the judge told her. 'If you want this medicine there is only one way you can have it. The medicine to make people like you is very difficult. And you must first bring me the milk from a wild buffalo.'

" 'It will be very difficult.' Abu rose from the mat where she'd been sitting. 'Too difficult. But I want this medicine more than anything else in the world. I want people to like me. And so, I will try—I'll try.'

"Early the next morning Abu left her compound to go into the bush to find a wild buffalo.

With her she took a big gourd full of grain. It was a long walk, and Abu was very tired by the time she came across the trail of the wild buffalo. The sun was high in the sky, and Abu was tired and discouraged. She was even more discouraged when the buffalo spotted her and thundered off into the bush. Abu poured out the grain onto the ground and returned home.

"Early the next morning Abu again started out to the bush. This time she took not only a gourd of grain but a small bag of salt. When she got out to the place where the wild buffalo were, she found that they had eaten the grain she'd poured out for them the day before. Once again she poured the grain on the ground and sprinkled the salt where the buffalo could see it.

Then Abu sat down in the shade of a tree and began to spin her thread. She sat very quietly all day long. The buffalo watched her from a distance but didn't come close to her.

"When the sun began to go down in the west, Abu picked up her thread and headed for home. The next day she repeated her performance and the next day and the next. Pretty soon the buffalo ceased running away when she would speak softly to them. Finally the buffalo would come

One day, Abu got close enough to actually touch the cow.

up to the grain and eat it and lick the salt while she was near. And one happy day Abu got close enough to one of the cows that she could actually touch her.

"But it was a long, weary process. Every so often Abu would almost forget how important the medicine would be to her, and she would be tempted to quit being kind to the buffalo."

"Being kind is awfully important," Baba told me. I squirmed. Baba wound some more of the dried grasses around his mat and pulled them tight. The mat was beginning to take shape. Being kind. Humph! Laraba should have been kind to me and let me come to the class feast. But— Well, maybe I should have been kind to her and helped her clean the schoolhouse. But, why should I help? It wasn't my feast.

Baba cleared his throat and went on with his story.

"One day Abu found that the wild buffalo were no longer wild. She could walk among them freely. She was nearly jumping with joy when she walked into the old judge's entrance hut with a gourd full of milk.

" 'Long life to you, Judge,' Abu said happily. 'Look, I have brought you the gourd full of milk from a wild buffalo. Now, I beg of you, give me the medicine to make people like me.'

" 'What did you do to get the milk from the wild bush cow?' the wise old judge asked her.

" 'I gave her things to eat that would please her. I tried to be kind to her. I helped her with salt, and I spoke kindly to her,' Abu answered.

" 'Go your way; you have the medicine,' the judge said."

"Baba," I said, jumping up from my shady place, "I've got to go down to the school. Will you excuse me, please? I want to help Laraba clean up the schoolhouse."

4

The Jackal and the Leopard

"Everybody's gone, and there's nothing to do," Little Lion complained.

"Why don't you practice with your bow and arrow?" I suggested. Little brothers can be so tiresome.

"Don't want to," he muttered.

"Well, why don't you go fishing?"

"Don't want to."

"Why don't you help me spin thread?"

"That's girl's work! *Haba!*" He sounded so disgusted.

"Well, quit grumbling and do something," I told him as I reached for some more cotton. It's fun to spin thread. I held the short piece of the cornstalk with the fuzzy white cotton on it in my left hand and twisted a little bit of the cotton into a thread. Then I fastened the thread to my spindle which I held in my right hand. I gave the spindle a twist. It keeps pulling the cotton out and spins it into a thread. Of course, sometimes my thread has lumps and bumps in it, but Baba says I'm learning real well.

"I'm lonesome," Little Lion fussed.

"Where's everyone gone?" I asked.

"Audu went to the market with his father. Ali went out to his peanut patch. Idi has to help his father mix mud for their house. And everybody's gone, and I'm lonesome."

"Once upon a time there was a lonesome jackal." I hadn't seen Baba coming. But, there he was, standing right behind us.

"Oh, Baba!" Little Lion jumped up and down. "Tell us about the lonesome jackal."

"Get your whittling knife and start working on this stool, and I'll tell you a story while you work. It is not good for us to sit here with our tongues busy and our hands idle," Baba said.

Little Lion ran into the house and came out with his whittling knife. Baba handed him a piece of wood. Because it was very soft and quite damp, it was easy to carve. Baba says all boys should learn a good trade. Our people have always been wood-carvers. Of course, my father preaches and farms too. But he's a very good wood-carver, just like Baba is.

Soon we were all quite busy. I was spinning, Little Lion was carving, and Baba was weaving a little *faifai* mat.

"Now tell us the story of the lonely jackal," Little Lion reminded Baba.

Baba tugged at his gray beard and reached into his deep pocket and chose a piece of colored grass for the mat. And then he began his story.

"Once upon a time, a long, long time ago, there was a lonely jackal. Now, this jackal was a very good hunter, but he was quite lonely.

" 'Oh, oh, oh, it is a pity!' he would howl every night. 'I wish I had someone to visit with me. I wish I had a friend. I wish I had someone to help me hunt. I wish I had someone to know how smart I am. Why, I am the smartest jackal in the whole wide world.'

"In the same bush land lived a leopard. Now, this leopard was also a very fine hunter. Every day he would find plenty of meat. But this leopard was lonely too.

"Every day he would go back to his sleeping place and would growl, 'I wish I had someone to visit with. I wish I had someone to talk to me. It is a pity that I can't tell someone how very clever I was today. It would be nice to have someone here to listen to me tell them how brave and strong I am.'

"Then the poor leopard would turn around and around and around and get his sleeping place smooth, and he would lie down for the night. But even his dreams were lonely.

"At the same time the lonely jackal would be stirring in his sleep and dreaming of having a friend.

"One day, early in the morning, the leopard set out for a hunting trip. He was so sad and lonely that he didn't pay much attention to where he was going. And so, after just catching one very small rabbit, he lay down in the shade of a tree. He ate his rabbit slowly. He was so unhappy that even rabbit, which he generally just loved, didn't taste very good.

" 'Oh, dear,' he growled, 'I wish I weren't so lonely. I wish I had someone here to listen to me tell how big and brave I am. I'd like to tell them about this very fine rabbit I just ate. Maybe it would have tasted better if I could have talked about it.'

"On the other side of the tree the poor lonely

jackal was resting. He, too, had been crying about his loneliness. He, too, had been wishing for someone to praise him. At first, when he heard the leopard growling, he was afraid. But then, slowly, he approached the leopard and began to talk to him.

"They soon became fast friends, and both of them went off to their homes and gathered up their belongings, and then set out to find a suitable place for them to live together.

"Finally they found a nice cave, and they set up housekeeping. Everything was very happy for several days. The jackal listened to the leopard boast about his cleverness and his bravery. The leopard listened to the jackal boast about how smart he was. They were very happy together until one day the leopard returned from hunting with a goat, and the jackal brought home a cow!

"When the leopard saw that the jackal had been more successful than he had been in his hunting, he was so embarrassed that he felt like digging a hole and crawling into it!

"However, the leopard didn't let the jackal know he was embarrassed about his poor hunting. After a long time the jackal finally went to sleep. The leopard was too unhappy to sleep. And so, in the middle of the night, the leopard got up and went outside to see if he couldn't make some kind of a plan that would show the jackal who was the cleverest and the bravest and the smartest. He thought of the scrawny little goat he'd caught and the nice big cow the jackal had caught, and he just felt so sad he wanted to cry.

" 'Why, everybody knows the leopard is a better hunter than the jackal,' he told himself as he crawled out of his nice warm cave.

"But, can you imagine how surprised and unhappy he was when he looked at the jackal's cow and saw that she had given birth to a very fine calf? Indeed, now it seemed that the leopard's shame was more than he could stand.

"The poor leopard began to pace back and forth in front of the cow and her calf. How unhappy he was! What could he do?

"All of a sudden, he had a brilliant idea. He crept over to the cow and snatched the young calf away. The leopard carried the calf to the side of the goat, who allowed the calf to nurse her.

"The leopard watched the goat and the calf

for a while, and then, smiling happily, he turned back into his cave and went to bed. He fell asleep with a happy grin around his whiskers.

"The next morning the jackal got up early to see how his cow was getting along. He hurried out of the cave and howled in anger when he saw the leopard's goat suckling a young calf.

"The leopard had crept out of the cave and was just behind the jackal. When the jackal turned around to storm into the cave, the leopard grinned. "Well, well, well. Now, isn't that wonderful? My goat has given birth to a calf!"

" 'So this is the way you treat me!' the jackal howled. 'You know very well that is my calf. You know my cow gave birth to that calf. It's mine, I tell you, it's mine!'

" 'Don't be silly,' the leopard purred. 'Don't you see where the calf is nursing, and where she slept all night? Of course the calf is my calf. My goat gave birth to it last night!'

"Oh, such an argument those two had! The jackal howled and the leopard growled, and both claimed the young calf.

"Finally, the jackal said, 'Well, we're not getting anything solved at this rate. I say it's mine, and you say it's yours. What we need is an honest and true judge. Come along with me to the forest and we'll find someone who can settle this thing for us.'

" 'It's silly to waste all this time,' the leopard complained. 'However, just to prove to you that my goat gave birth to the calf, we'll go find a judge.' "

Baba stopped talking and leaned over to help Little Lion with his carving. You could begin to see a leg of a stool taking shape.

"You know what the story reminds me of?" I asked Baba.

"No, what does it remind you of, Sunday?"

"Well, it's like Father was saying in his sermon the other day. He said a mango tree wouldn't have thorns because it was a mango tree. And he said a thorn tree couldn't have mangoes because it's a thorn tree. He said we couldn't be called the children of God unless we really were His children. We have to believe on the Lord Jesus. That's silly, saying you're a Christian, if you don't love the Lord Jesus. And it's silly thinking a goat could have a calf. It sure won't take a very smart judge to answer that for them!"

Little Lion tossed some of the wood shavings into the fire. They were wet and they spit and sputtered in the flames.

Baba added another piece of grass to his *faifai* mat and went on with his story.

"And so, the leopard and the jackal started out to look for a judge. The very first animal they met was a rabbit.

" 'Mr. Rabbit,' the leopard said, 'we've come to ask you to be our judge.'

" 'You mean—you mean *you* want me, a poor little scared rabbit, to judge between a leopard and a jackal? No thanks! I've no wish to be caught between the jaws of either a jackal or a leopard. I'm getting out of here!' Poor Mr. Rabbit shook with fear.

"But finally, after much persuasion, the rabbit agreed to listen to the argument of the leopard and the jackal.

"The poor frightened rabbit sat there shaking and trembling while he listened to the story, first from the jackal, and then from the leopard.

"As soon as the rabbit had heard their stories, he jumped up and started hopping off. Looking back over his shoulder, his nose quivering with fear, the scared little rabbit called out, 'Fine,

fine, I've heard your stories. It is fine. If you say the goat gave birth to a calf, who am I to argue? I agree. I agree. I heartily agree! Good-bye!' And before the jackal or the leopard could even answer him, he'd scampered away and disappeared down his burrow.

"The leopard turned to the jackal. 'Now, you see, I am right. The rabbit said I was right!'

" 'Let's go find another judge,' the jackal howled.

"They went on a little farther and found a small monkey in a tree. The leopard growled at the little monkey, 'We've come for you to judge for us. Who's right? The jackal? Or am I right?'

" 'W-w-w-well,' chattered the frightened little monkey, 'how would I know who's right? What's wrong? Anyhow, I don't want to judge between. you two. A monkey—a little tiny monkey—judge a leopard? Or a jackal? Don't be silly! I don't want to be your dinner.'

"But finally the monkey agreed to listen to their stories, but only from the safe distance of the high tree. And then, he did just as the rabbit had done.

" 'I agree, I fully agree. The leopard is the

biggest, and I agree with him,' the monkey called out as he scampered up to the highest branch he could find.

" 'Now, it is settled. It has really been decided who is right.' The leopard purred with pleasure.

" 'No! Let's go on. I'm sure we'll find an honest judge somewhere. After all, they can't all be afraid of us. Surely there is someone who isn't afraid to judge rightly. I know, let's go find the gorilla. He's the strongest animal in the forest.'

"The leopard gulped. 'But—but, the gorilla can tear me in two with one hand!'

" 'That's exactly my point,' the jackal said. 'The gorilla won't be afraid of either of us. He will judge wisely because he isn't afraid. After all, neither of us could even catch him. And if we tried, he'd tear us limb from limb.'

" 'Well, I don't think it's fair,' the leopard growled. 'We've had two judges and I'm right.'

" 'And now we're going to an honest judge,' the jackal insisted and led the leopard into the forest in search of a gorilla.

"Finally they found a huge gorilla. Bravely, the jackal approached the gorilla. 'Long life to

"The leopard is the biggest and I agree with him."

you, sir. If you please, sir, we are searching for a true and an honest judge. Will you listen to our story and tell us who is right?'

"The gorilla agreed to listen and they told him the story of the goat and the cow. The gorilla called one of his children. 'Son,' he said, 'go and get me a couple of grinding stones, a big one and a little one.'

"The leopard and the jackal looked at each other in amazement. What could the gorilla want with grinding stones?

"The young gorilla went off in search of the stones, and in a few minutes was back with the two stones. The gorilla took the stones and sat down on a fallen tree trunk. He didn't look at either the jackal or the leopard. He just took a stone in each hand and began to rub them together.

"The jackal and the leopard watched him silently for a few minutes. Then they looked at each other, and back to the gorilla.

" 'You know, I think he's ignoring us,' the leopard whispered.

" 'No,' answered the jackal, 'I think maybe he didn't understand what we were talking about.'

"Then the jackal turned to the gorilla. 'If you please, sir. We have come for you to settle our argument.'

" 'I'm settling it,' the gorilla roared.

" 'But, please, sir, we are—we see you're just sitting there—not doing anything, not saying anything. You are just ignoring us,' the leopard complained.

" 'I'm not ignoring you,' the gorilla answered. 'I'm playing my musical instruments. I am waiting for my musical instruments to sing. When I've finished listening to the music, then I'll answer you.'

"The leopard screamed, 'What! Those aren't musical instruments! They are grinding stones! Whoever heard music come from a grinding stone?'

"Then the wise old gorilla smiled. 'Well,' he said softly, 'if you haven't heard music from a grinding stone, then the day a goat gives birth to a calf, that is the day you'll hear music from a stone.'

"The leopard knew that he was caught. He knew the wise old gorilla wouldn't stand for any more lies. He hung his head and said, 'The calf is yours. I'm sorry.' Then the leopard and the jackal said good-bye to the gorilla and went on their way."

I laughed. "Oh, Baba, that was a funny story. Look, Little Lion. Here comes Audu back with his father."

Little Lion tossed his knife down and ran out to meet his friend.

"Guess he won't be lonesome now," I muttered as I spun my thread. It was good thread.

5

The Poor Woodchopper

"You'd never think this funny-looking stuff would make nice strong rope," I told Baba.

I was helping him strip the bark off our big monkey-bread tree. Baba would make a cut across the tree as high up as he could reach, and then I would very carefully work my fingers under the cut and pull the bark down. I was standing on Mother's pounding mortar so I could reach high. I had to be very careful not to break the bark off short. Baba wanted nice long strips.

I held a strip of the bark in my hand. It was fragile-looking. It didn't look like it would hold anything. But I knew that after Baba had worked on it that it would be strong and pliable.

We call the monkey-bread tree "Joy Tree"

because it does so many things for us. We children eat the sweet white fruit. Mother uses the white fruit after it has been dried and pounded to mix into the food she cooks. She also uses the leaves for seasoning in our gravy.

We make rope out of the bark. It doesn't hurt the tree to have the bark stripped off; it just grows more bark for us. And then, finally, when the tree gets old and dies, we use the wood for fire. So you can see, it really is a "Joy Tree."

But it isn't a pretty tree. I looked at the gnarled, stubby branches.

"Baba, why is it so ugly?" I asked.

"Well, Sunday, I don't really think that anything as useful as this tree is really ugly. But look at that nice-looking green tree over there. Doesn't it look soft and nice? Do you like it better?"

"I sure don't!" I laughed. "That tree looks pretty—from a nice long distance. But, you get close, and you really get stuck. Those thorns! They hurt."

"It's a lot like people," Baba said. He was working the bark between his fingers to make it nice and soft. "Some people look fine and good, but their hearts are thorny."

I was moving the pounding mortar back by our house when I saw Little Lion struggling up the path with a big load of wood on his head.

"Better run and help him," Baba told me. I put a big round *faifai* mat over the top of the mortar so that the chickens wouldn't try to get in and look for food. Then I ran down the path to Little Lion.

"Haba!" I told him. "You've really worked hard." I helped him slip the big bundle of wood off his head, and together we carried it to the woodpile near our house.

"Bet I'm the best woodchopper in town," Little Lion bragged as he wiped the sweat off his forehead.

"I don't see how you carried it at all. Did you really chop it yourself?" I asked.

"Well, Father chopped the big branches off the trees. Then, when they fell to the ground, I chopped all these little branches off them. But, if you chop enough little ones, you get a nice big pile of wood. Pretty good, huh? But I am tired!" Little Lion plunked himself right down on the ground.

"Very good," Baba said as he came up behind us. "Well, I think you've earned a rest—and some spending money." Baba reached into the long, deep pocket in front of his gown. "Here's a *taro* for you," he said as he tossed a shiny coin to Little Lion.

"Oh, Baba! Three pence!" Little Lion seemed to forget he was tired as he jumped off the ground and started swinging his little ax.

"Watch out or you'll chop your ears off," Baba laughed. Then he turned to me. "And here's three pence for you, too, Sunday. This is for working so hard and pulling the bark off the Joy Tree. And also for helping your mother pound grain this morning. Now, I think both of you have earned a rest. Sit down, and I'll tell you a story about a woodchopper."

"About me?" Little Lion asked.

"No, not about you," Baba laughed as he pulled the lion-skin mat out of its storage place in the branches of the tree right by our doorway.

"No, this story is about another woodchopper. This woodchopper hid his money in an earthen pot in the ground."

"Hope nobody stole it, 'cause that's just exactly where I'm going to hide mine." Little Lion yawned.

"No, no one stole his money," Baba said. "I think your money will be safe."

Little Lion stretched out on the mat in front of us. He'd done a lot of work for a little six-year-old boy.

Baba picked up another piece of bark and began to work it slowly between his fingers. "Once upon a time, a long, long time ago, there was a poor but honest woodchopper whose name was Shehu," Baba began his story.

"Every morning, long before the sun was up, Shehu would get up off his sleeping mat. He'd warm over a bit of the porridge he had left from the night before, hastily eat it, and then hurry off to the bush. He'd be chopping wood a long time before any of his neighbors were out of bed.

"Shehu, like most of the people in his town, was very poor. Their farms were very poor farms, far from the town. The chief of the village owned all the good farms close to the village.

"Taxes were high in the village and, one by one, the chief had claimed all the nearby farms to pay for the taxes. Of course, nobody blamed the chief for the high taxes. 'It's what the sacred goat demands,' the chief told the people. The village chief was very generous with gifts to the poor townspeople. Quite often he would give one of the beggars one of his old discarded robes. And it wasn't uncommon at all to find a line of beggars outside his house every evening waiting for the scraps out of the chief's cooking pots.

"Shehu had often dreamed of being rich like the chief. 'He must be really good and smart to be so rich,' Shehu would tell himself.

"And so poor Shehu, like the other poor people of the town, worked and dreamed of the time when he, too, would be rich. But although all the poor people worked very hard, nobody worked harder than Shehu, the woodchopper.

"He walked many miles every day in search of wood. He'd load his little donkey with wood, and then carry another load on his own head."

Little Lion twisted into a more comfortable position on the mat.

"Wish I'd had a donkey today," he muttered. "Maybe I'll save my money and buy a donkey. Then I can make lots of money by bringing wood in to sell."

"Quit dreaming about getting rich," I said, "and let Baba finish the story."

Baba went on with his story. "On his way home every afternoon, Shehu would stop at his little peanut patch and spend two or three hours hoeing the weeds. Then he'd put the wood back on his donkey, pick up his own head load of wood and, shortly after sunset, he would get back into the village.

"But his work was not over yet. He'd take the wood into the little marketplace in the center of town and sell it. He would arrange the wood into neat little bundles. Some he'd sell for half a penny, some for a penny, and some for three pennies.

"Then, when he'd sold all but one large bundle of wood, he would go by the chief's house and give him the load of wood that the chief demanded for the privilege of using the marketplace. Shehu would look around at the fine furnishings and would long for the day when he could have a fine house. Sometimes the chief would give him a present: a small bowl of grain, or even a penny for the wood. Then Shehu would think how wonderful it was that they had a chief who was so generous and good.

"Of course, the poor people of the town couldn't afford to pay much for the wood that

Shehu brought in. But, because Shehu spent very little money on food, and even less on clothes, he soon had a fairly good supply of pennies and *taros*. This money he hid away in a small earthen pot in the ground under his sleeping mat.

"Because there was so very much thievery in town, Shehu was always very careful never to tell anyone about his growing supply of money. When he would get four *taros*, he would ask someone to give him a shilling for them. But, he would never ask the same person twice in a row, and so no one ever suspected that the poor woodchopper had even saved a penny.

"Didn't they have any policemen?" Little Lion rolled over and looked up at Baba. "I bet Constable Sule would have caught those thieves."

"No, there weren't any policemen," Baba answered. "You see, this story happened a long, long time ago, before there were policemen like we have now. In those days, the chief and his men were the only law that the town had.

"Well, as I said, Shehu saved his money and hid it away. It wasn't that he was a miser. He had a very special plan for his money.

"One night after the whole town was sound asleep, Shehu lit his little oil lamp and dug into the ground under his bed. He pulled out his earthen pot and started to count his money.

" 'Forty pounds, forty-five pounds, forty-six, forty-seven, forty-eight, forty-nine—fifty!' Shehu almost shouted with joy. 'Well,' he said to himself, 'it looks like I've finally gotten all the money I need. Now I shall go to my father's village and claim my bride. I shall pay her dowry and then I will buy fine things for our house. Ah, yes, I have worked long and hard. Now I shall have a good wife and a decent house.'

"It was late that night before Shehu finally fell asleep. Early the next morning he tied his money up in two small bags and hid it under a little load of wood. He put on his best gown and started out toward his father's village.

"Even the little donkey seemed to sense Shehu's joyful mood and needed no prodding as it trotted merrily on its way.

"The two-day trip seemed more like two hours to Shehu because of the joy in his heart. He sang as he walked along the sandy path beside his little donkey:

Poor Shehu is a rich man now,
For many years he's slaved,
To get the money that he has,
For many years he's saved.

"Of course, there was much rejoicing when Shehu returned safely to his father's village. All his old friends were glad to see him. But, when he told them that he'd come to claim his bride, there was really a big celebration with much drumming and feasting. Everyone was so happy for him because they all knew he had worked hard and long to save his money.

"Shehu paid the bride-price and spent the rest of the money buying fine mats and pots for his new wife. He bought several bolts of cloth and some good brassware. He bought bottles of perfume and some very fine cushions. Shehu's new wife was very happy. She knew that he had saved all this money so that he could give her fine gifts.

"After the marriage feast was over, they loaded the faithful little donkey with all the fine gifts their friends had given them. These, with the bolts of cloth and pots and lovely gifts that Shehu had bought, were almost as heavy as some

They made many plans as they walked to their village.

of the loads of wood that the poor donkey had had to carry.

"All the way back to their village Shehu kept telling his bride about his little house and their village. 'Oh, it's not a fine big house like the chief has; he's got a fine palace. But, my house is sturdy, and the grass roof doesn't leak. Everyone has to work hard. There is only one thing wrong with our village. Someone is a thief. Nobody seems to know who it is. The chief has looked and looked, but he hasn't been able to catch the thief. Well, one thing, with you home all day long, no one will be able to take our lovely gifts.'

"They made many plans as they walked back to their village. When they arrived in the little town it was quite late at night. Everyone was sound asleep. The only person they saw as they led the heavily laden donkey through the quiet paths of the town was the village chief. He was sitting outside his fine house.

" 'Ah, good evening. Long life to you, Chief,' Shehu greeted him. 'I have just come back from my father's village. And I have brought myself a wife back with me. Yes, and all these fine goods that I bought and that my friends gave us. We will have a very comfortable house now. It will be good to have a wife to cook for me.'

" 'Wedding presents, huh?' the old chief grunted as he got up off his soft leather cushions. 'Did you get a lot of nice gifts?'

" 'Ah, yes. Long life to you, Chief,' Shehu answered. 'We will be very happy. We have some fine brass dishes, several bolts of cloth, some nice enameled pans—lots of good things. Yes, I have lived miserably long enough. Now I shall enjoy myself. Oh, I will keep on working hard and chopping wood and farming. But we will live well.'

" 'Speaking of farming,' the old chief said, 'I have some bad news for you. I just heard this evening that monkeys have been raiding your peanut farm. If I were you, I'd go right out and guard my farm tonight. Now that you have a wife to take care of, you can't afford to lose a good peanut crop like yours.'

" 'Oh, what a pity!' poor Shehu groaned. 'It would be a shame to lose that crop after I've worked so hard.'

" 'Yes,' the old chief agreed, 'it would be a pity. I'd hurry right out there if I were you and keep the monkeys off. You can't afford not to do this.'

" 'Oh, dear,' Shehu sighed. 'Well, I'd better hurry. It's late. I'll have to get my wife settled down first. And, it's so far out to my farm. Good-bye, Chief. It was very kind of you to tell me about the monkeys.'

"With this, Shehu and his wife hurried down the path to their little house.

"Shehu's wife was very pleased when she saw her little home. But as soon as Shehu had unloaded the donkey and piled the wedding presents in a heap on the floor, he started out to his farm. He had only reached his gateway when he turned back to his house.

" 'You know, Wife, I'm just too tired to go out to the farm tonight. We've walked many miles today. No, if the monkeys have been there for a couple of nights now, they must have eaten everything up anyhow. I'm just too tired —I can't go. I will sleep tonight. If the peanuts are gone, they are gone. It is too bad, but I'm too tired.' "

I nudged Baba and pointed to Little Lion. He was lying there on the mat sound asleep.

Too much woodchopping to even listen to the story.

"Someone else is tired, too," I said. "Well, I'm not tired. Tell me the rest."

Baba lowered his voice and continued. "It didn't take Shehu long to unroll his sleeping mat and spread it out on the floor beside his wife. In a very few moments he was sound asleep.

"A couple of hours passed by. Shehu and his wife slept on. It was very dark in the hut. And quiet, except for the heavy breathing of Shehu and his wife. But then, the mat that hung in the doorway was softly pushed to one side. A dark form entered the hut. Shehu stirred in his sleep. Something brushed lightly across his face. He groaned and turned over. Another dark figure entered the hut."

Baba's soft voice and the scary story made my head prickle. I huddled closer to Baba. The sun was setting, and maybe it was the cold air that made little duck bumps on my arms.

Baba said, "Shehu slept soundly. Neither he nor his wife heard the soft laughter of the men who had entered their house.

" 'Ha!' one of the thieves said. 'Shehu won't

be home tonight. Only the wife is here. Shehu will be walking out to his farm to scare the monkeys off. Only, there aren't any monkeys. That's just a story I made up to get him away from home.' "

"Oh, Baba!" I cried, "it's the chief! He's the thief! Oh, how awful."

"Yes, Sunday." Baba motioned me to be quiet. I'd almost forgotten that Little Lion was asleep.

"The chief looked like a good man. He dressed fine and had nice clothes. He even gave food to beggars. But, it's just like we were saying earlier this evening. You can't tell by outward appearances. The monkey-bread bark doesn't look very good, but it's strong. The thorn tree looks soft and green, but it hurts. That's why it is so important to have our hearts right. Everyone looked up to the chief because he was the chief. You know, the Bible tells us that man looks on the outward appearances, but God looks on the heart."

Baba picked up another piece of bark and began to work it between his fingers. I waited anxiously to hear the end of the story.

"Another voice said, 'Well, it won't be any

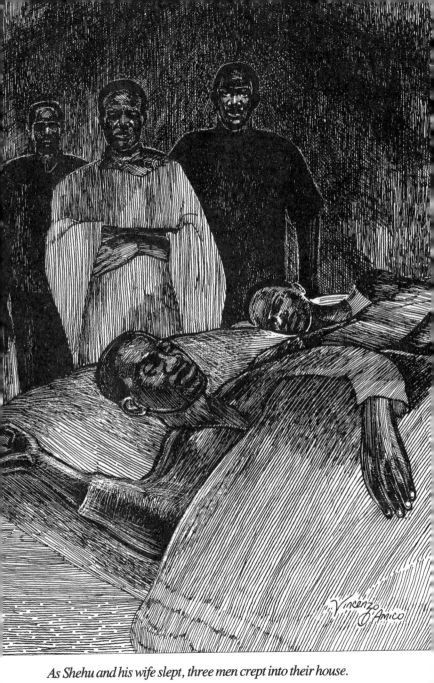

As Shehu and his wife slept, three men crept into their house.

trouble to rob just one woman. Softly now, softly, softly.'

"Suddenly there was a crash! *Bang!*

" 'By the horn of the trumpeter!' one of the thieves cursed, 'I've broken my toe! I bumped into something.'

"Shehu woke up with a start. 'What's that? What's the matter? Huh? Who's there?'

" 'It's Shehu. Tie him up!' a rough voice commanded.

"Another voice growled, 'He shouldn't be here. Why, he lied!'

"Poor Shehu was too upset and frightened and half groggy with sleep to be sure just what was going on. The three thieves soon overpowered him, and poor Shehu and his wife were bound with ropes and then gagged.

"The thieves then picked up all the presents and carried them out of poor Shehu's little house.

"Shehu and his wife wiggled and twisted all night long. You can imagine how Shehu felt. All the years he'd struggled and saved—and now, in one night, everything gone!

"About six o'clock in the morning, Shehu finally managed to get an arm free. It didn't take him long to undo the rest of his bonds and to free his wife.

"As soon as they were loose, they hurried down the path to the chief's house to complain to him that thieves had stolen all their wedding gifts.

"But as they neared the chief's compound, they heard angry voices quarreling.

" 'It's mine, I tell you. I should have the biggest share.'

" 'No, mine is the largest share,' another voice complained.

" 'Both of you stop fighting!' This voice sounded vaguely familiar to Shehu. He stopped and grabbed his wife before she could enter the compound.

"The first voice cried out, 'I had to tie Shehu up. He fought very hard. That's why I should have the most of the lot.'

" 'But,' answered the voice that Shehu now recognized, 'I planned the whole business just like I've planned all of them before. And I get the biggest share. Can I help it because he didn't go out to the farm?'

"Quickly Shehu began to scream and cry. He

set up a hue and cry that brought all the townspeople to the chief's doorway.

" 'Look! Look! Those are *my* goods. Those
are *my* wedding presents—*my* dishes, *my* brassware, *my* cushions and bolts of cloth and bottles
of perfume,' he cried.

"The chief and his two thieves were caught.
They had no way to escape. Happily, Shehu and
his wife gathered up their wedding presents and
returned home rejoicing.

"Word reached the ears of the sultan, and the
town's chief was put into prison.

"One day Shehu was very much surprised to
see a messenger from the sultan appear at his
doorway.

" 'Greetings,' the red-turbaned messenger said
to Shehu, 'I have come from the sultan. The
sultan, long life to him, has appointed you to be
chief of the town.' "

"Oh, Baba!" I clapped my hands. "How nice
for Shehu! I'm glad he got his things back, and
that he was made chief. Imagine a woodchopper
getting to be chief of a town."

"I'm going to be chief someday," Little Lion
muttered sleepily.

6

The Rat-Catcher's Son

"I don't know which one I like best."

I looked at the lovely strings of beads. They were so beautiful. There was one string of beads that was brown and white. And another that was green and white; and the third, all blue.

Abu Bakar had told me I could choose one string for my very own. Abu Bakar makes beads. Beautiful ones. The reason he said I could choose a string of beads for my very own was that I'd been collecting bottles for him. He makes these beads out of bottles. It's lots of fun to watch him heat the glass and twist the soft, hot pieces of glass into lovely beads. I'd brought him a lot of empty bottles—green ones, white ones, blue ones.

"Baba." I turned to my grandfather. "Which one do you like best?"

"You're the one who's going to wear them, Sunday." Baba laughed. "I don't think I'd look very good with a string of beads around my neck."

"But you must help me decide," I said.

Baba poked at the fire with his stick. The flames leaped high—and then died down to a soft reddish glow. The coals looked like bright red beads. I wished I'd found some red bottles. I'd like to have a string of red beads. The beads I held in my hands sparkled in the firelight. They all looked so pretty. The brown and white ones looked almost red in the firelight.

"Choices," Baba whispered softly. "Choices, every moment of the day, choices."

I nodded in agreement. "Like choosing which beads I want. It's awfully hard to make up my mind. They all look so nice."

I sat down beside Baba. It was so nice and warm by the fire. The sun had been hot all day, but here on the edge of the desert it gets cold just as soon as the sun goes down.

I laid the beads down on the lion-skin mat and looked at them. I'd just about chosen the brown beads. They looked so lovely in the firelight.

"No," Baba said softly, "I can't really decide for you. I could tell you which ones I liked best. But, in the end, you must make your own decision.

"There're a lot of decisions people have to make," Baba said. It was almost like he really wasn't talking to me, more like he was talking to himself. "Choices—every day brings dozens of choices: what to wear, what to eat, what to say. But, Sunday, these aren't really important decisions!'

"But, Baba," I complained, "it's awfully important for me to choose the right string of beads."

"Yes, Sunday, I know. But there's another decision that everyone must make. It's one choice that can mean—does mean—the difference between life and death."

"Oh, you sound serious." I shivered.

"I *am* serious," Baba said.

"About what?" I asked.

"Well, Sunday, you've already made this decision. You chose Jesus Christ as your Saviour. And you chose the right way. But everyone must make this decision for himself. No one can force another person to make it; everyone must choose for himself."

I picked up the green beads. They were pretty too.

"One time there was a mean old man named Bunu," Baba said.

I pulled my cloth up around my shoulders and snuggled down on the mat close beside Grandfather. I knew there was an interesting story coming. Baba knows such good stories.

"Bunu and his son, Gero, were very, very poor. The only trade they knew was rat-catching. They would go out into the farmlands and into the bush around the farms and catch rats. They would then take them into the town and sell the rats to other people for meat. They were so very poor that if on any one day they didn't catch any rats, that was the day they had nothing to eat.

"Well," Baba continued, "early one morning Bunu woke up. He was cold and hungry. Last night's supper had been one very small rat and a few roasted peanuts they'd swept up off the ground in the market.

" 'Come on!' Bunu kicked his son Gero. 'Get up off the mat and stir your lazy bones. If you hadn't been so slow yesterday, we'd have caught more rats. Now, get up and quit your fussing.' And he kicked poor Gero again.

"Gero got up from his ragged sleeping mat. He was cold and stiff and very hungry.

" 'Father,' he groaned, 'isn't there anything to eat? I tried yesterday. Honestly, I did. I dug very deep and very hard. But, I couldn't find any more rats. And I'm so cold. You've got the only blanket—'

" 'You're a lazy, worthless son. If you'd looked harder and run faster you could have caught another rat yesterday. And besides, I'm your father and it is only right that I have the blanket. You're just a boy—and a good-for-nothing one, at that.'

"Big tears rolled down Gero's pinched little cheeks. He rubbed his eyes, leaving dusty streaks across his dirty face. He wished his mother were still alive. Maybe he'd have someone who loved him then.

"He got up off his ragged straw mat, rolled the mat up, and tied it with a piece of rag. Getting dressed was no problem for little Gero. He twisted the old ragged cloth that he wore around his waist into a tighter knot and followed his father out to the farmlands.

"They walked miles and miles that day, and little Gero was faint with hunger by the time they came upon a large rathole late that afternoon. Bunu dug down into the hole and finally caught a nice fat rat.

" 'Here, Gero, hold this rat tightly. And don't let it go, or I'll beat you. I think there's another rat down this hole. If I get two rats, I shall feast well tonight. I can eat one and sell the other one for at least three pence.'

"Bunu shoveled the ground away from the rathole and continued planning. 'Yes, if I get three pence for the rat, I can buy me a nice bowlful of porridge.'

"Little Gero knew better than to ask if he was going to share that bowl of porridge. All he could do was to hope his father would let him scrape the porridge dish when he was finished eating.

"Sweat was pouring off Bunu's forehead when he finally yelled out, 'There, I've got him—a nice fat one. Well, that's good. I eat tonight.'

"But just as he said this, the second big rat

wiggled out of his hands and scampered across the rough field.

"Gero saw the nice fat rat getting away; he raced across the field to catch it for his father. But poor Little Gero tripped over a stone and fell—kerplop—right on his face! And the big fat rat he was holding in his arms flew out of his grasp and scooted away."

I gasped. "Oh, Baba, what happened to him then? Poor Gero! I'll bet his father beat him."

"That's just what mean old Bunu did," Baba told me. "He took a stick and began beating little Gero. He beat him and beat him. At first Gero's screams were loud and clear, but after a few minutes he gave a little moan and dropped to the ground.

"Mean old Bunu looked down at his son. 'Well, I guess I've killed him,' he said. Bunu tossed his stick away and turned back toward town. 'Just as well, I won't have to bother feeding him. He was clumsy and worthless anyway. Now, I guess I'd better try to find me another rat.' "

"Oh, Baba did he go off and leave poor Gero just like that?" I cried.

"So he did, Sunday, so he did." Baba shook

his head. "You see, Bunu's heart was mean and wicked. He had made a decision. He had decided to live only for himself, and he had no love in his heart."

"Is that the big decision you said we have to make, Baba?"

"No, not really, Sunday. That's only part of the decision. That's what you might call the fruit of the decision. Let me explain. The biggest decision a person will ever have to make is to answer the question, 'What will I do with Jesus?' If a person decides to accept the Lord Jesus as his Saviour and to love Him and follow Him, then he will try to live for others and to help others. But the biggest decision—the most important decision a person will ever have to make in his life—is to decide what he will do with the Lord Jesus."

I picked up the string of brown beads. The firelight shone red on them. "I'm glad I've decided the right way—glad I made my decision to follow the Lord Jesus and to love Him," I whispered.

Baba stirred the fire again. He sat quietly for a minute and I was almost afraid he'd forgotten to finish the story. He sighed, tugged at his beard, and began again.

"Yes, Bunu chose evil. He went off and left his son lying on the ground. Shortly after Bunu left, a rich man named Idirisu came along the path. Idirisu was the richest man in the country. This day he was riding his favorite horse, a fine black one. Idirisu had many servants with him. When he saw poor Gero lying there on the ground, he galloped away from his servants and hurried over to where Gero lay quietly.

"At first Idirisu thought the boy was dead. *'Wai!* This poor child,' Idirisu cried. 'He has been sorely beaten. It looks like he—I am sure he is dead. *Wayyo! Wayyo!* But—no! Wait! I think I saw him stir!'

"Kind Idirisu's hands were shaking with nervousness as he lifted poor Gero's head. 'Here, bring me some water,' he commanded his servants.

"After a while Gero stirred and moaned in pain. A little while later he regained consciousness. Although he tried to be brave, he could not help but shed a few tears because of his many wounds.

"Carefully Idirisu lifted Gero up onto his

Shortly after Banu left, a rich man named Idirisu came along the path

horse and held him gently until they had reached the town where Idirisu lived.

"Everyone was quite surprised when Idirisu arrived home with a young boy and told the townspeople that from now on Gero would be known as his son. The rich man treated Gero with loving-kindness and gave him everything he needed and wanted. He also taught him to be honest and truthful and helpful to all people. The townspeople were quite amazed at Idirisu's taking in a strange young boy.

" 'If he ever wastes any of Idirisu's money or does any damage, I'll bet he'll beat him and turn him out to beg!' some of them said.

"Others said, 'No, Idirisu is a just and kind man. He won't treat Gero like that!'

"This argument between the townspeople went on for two or three years. Gero learned to love and trust Idirisu and he was growing into a fine young man. But one day Idirisu learned that the townspeople were arranging a cruel test of his love. He learned that they were still doubting his love for Gero and that they had decided to test both him and Gero.

"So Idirisu called Gero and warned him that the townspeople were going to test him. 'And,'

Idirisu warned, 'you must be careful to do everything just exactly like the other boys do. Do everything they do. Do not consider me or my feelings at all. I want the townspeople to know you are just as dear to me as though you were my actual son.'

"That afternoon the sons of the other rich men in town invited Gero to go horseback riding with them. When they arrived at a small village, all the other boys gave away their fine clothes and money to the townspeople. Now, Gero's clothes were of the finest silk and velvet, much finer than any of the other boys' clothes. But, when he saw the other boys giving away their fine turbans and long robes, he too, gave his clothes away. And Gero gave away all of his money. His bag was much fuller than any of the other boys', but he gave it away, down to the last *anini*. He didn't keep even one-tenth of a penny for himself.

"Then the other boys got off of their fine horses and beat them and drove them off into the bush. 'Surely, Gero won't drive Idirisu's favorite black horse away,' they told one another.

"But Gero got off the fine black horse and

gave it a smack across the back and watched it as it trotted off into the wilderness.

" 'Truly, Gero is not afraid of Idirisu,' the boys said. 'Now, when we get back to our village we will see what Idirisu does when he finds out how Gero has given away his clothes and money and lost his fine black horse.'

"But, to their amazement, Idirisu merely called the best weaver in the town and had five new robes made for Gero. And he bought him three black horses on the next market day.

" 'Truly, by the beard of the sacred goat, we swear, this man Idirisu loves Gero,' the townspeople told one another.

"But one day Gero was called upon to make a choice—a very important choice. This choice would affect his life for the rest of his days.

"This day Gero was out riding on one of his new horses, and he met a man.

" 'I say, stranger,' Gero called out, 'you look familiar to me. What is your name?'

" 'Well, I *should* look familiar to you. I'm Bunu, your father. Hmm, I thought I'd killed you. Well, it's good you are alive. You can get busy and help me find rats to sell. But, where did you get those fine clothes?'

" 'Ever since you tried to kill me,' Gero said, 'I have been living with Idirisu. He is my new father, and he loves me. He treats me kindly. I am very happy with him.'

" 'Well,' Bunu whined, 'you are my son. And now I want you to come and live with me and catch rats. After all, I'm getting to be an old man now. You should be a good son and help your poor old father.'

" 'But, Father,' Gero cried, 'you almost killed me. And Idirisu has been a loving father to me.'

" 'You are my son, and I command you to come and help me dig rats. You must leave this man Idirisu who has stolen you away from me.'

"Gero argued and argued with Bunu, but all Bunu would do was to scream and fuss at him.

"Finally Gero said, 'Father, please come see Idirisu. I want you to talk to him. It is true that you are my father, but I love Idirisu very much. He has taught me to be kind and helpful. It would be hard to leave him.'

"Grumbling, fussing, and swearing, the dirty, ragged rat-catcher followed Gero to the fine home of Idirisu. Idirisu welcomed Bunu and gave him good food and a nice room to sleep in.

But Bunu was not satisfied. He demanded that Idirisu give him back his son. Bunu would listen to no reasoning at all.

" 'He is my son, my only son. I want him back. You've stolen my son!' Bunu screamed at kind old Idirisu.

" 'I did not steal him. I rescued him from death,' Idirisu argued. 'You beat him and left him to die in the wilderness. I came along on my horse and found him. You felt no pity for him. But, I wept when I thought he was dead. Even though I did not know him, I wept for him. And then, when I saw there remained a little life in him, I gave him water and medicine and tender love. I cared for him and nursed him until he was fine and strong and well. I have been the true father to him.'

"A sly look came into Bunu's eyes. He searched in the seam of his ragged robe for a louse, found it, and snapped it between his fingers.

"Gero drew closer to Idirisu. All the filth and dirt of the old rat-catcher was sickening to him. Idirisu put his hand upon Gero's shoulder.

"Bunu whined, 'You say you've taught him to be good and always do what is right? Well, is it not a custom of our people that a son should follow his father's trade? Is it not the custom of our people that a son should care for his aged father? I ask you, is this not true?'

" 'He shall take care of you,' Idirisu promised. 'You may live here in the house with us. All you need will be provided for you.'

" '*No!*' Bunu cursed. 'I want him all by myself. I do not intend to share him with you. I *like* catching rats. That is my trade. And that is what he shall do for a living. It is only fitting that a son should follow in his father's profession. No, he must leave you and live with me. I demand that you give me my son!'

"Poor Idirisu's shoulder sagged as he turned sadly away. 'Let us decide this in the morning,' he said. 'I leave you now.'

"Early the next morning Idirisu called Bunu and Gero and told them to follow him out to the farm. Idirisu had a long silver sword with him. When they reached the middle of the farm he handed the sword to Gero.

" 'Here, Gero, you take this sword. Now, you must decide between me and your father. If you want to live with me, take this sword and kill your father and come home with me. If you

"Now, you must decide between me and your father."

want to go with your father, take the sword and run it through my heart.'

" 'Oh, Idirisu, I love you. I couldn't do that!' Gero cried.

" 'There is no other way,' Idirisu said sadly. 'You must decide for yourself. No one can decide for you.'

" 'I couldn't kill you. I couldn't kill my father either. I would rather kill myself. I do not want the sword. I will tell you what I will do.'

"Gero looked at his father. 'Father,' he said, 'I was your son, but you never treated me as your son. You never showed love toward me and you often beat me. Often I was given nothing to eat, and I was always cold at night because you did not share your blanket. When you whipped me and thought that I had died, you went away and left me without a tear.'

"Then Gero looked at Idirisu. 'You have treated me as your son,' he said. 'When I was beaten and near death, you rescued me. You have given me clothes and a fine home and many other things. But most important you have always loved me, even when I gave away my clothes and money and lost your fine black horse.

I have made my decision. I will stay with you. You are my real father.' "

Baba leaned toward the fire. "Gero had to make his own decision, just like we must make ours."

I picked up the brown beads that shone blood-red in the firelight. "Baba," I said softly, "I'm awfully glad that I have chosen to follow the Lord Jesus."

7

The Ungrateful Beggar

"What's the matter, Sunday?" Baba was sitting on the lion-skin mat. He was making a new little grass mat for Mother.

"Oh, nothing," I sighed as I tossed a little twig into the fire. Mother and Father were already asleep in their room. Little Lion was sound asleep too. Only Baba and I were still up. It was dark, but I like sitting by the fire at night. It's quiet then and I can think about my problems. I've got lots of problems. I just don't think Mother and Father understand.

It's nice to be a Christian. But, *haba!* Father just doesn't understand. I like going to church and Sunday school. We have lots of fun. And I like singing the choruses and saying the Bible verses. It's good to know that the Lord Jesus loves me. I like that song, "Jesus loves me, this I know, for the Bible tells me so."

But, well, I just don't see why I have to walk that long way into Market Town just because the older folks are going. If they were going to the market and I could see all the sights—the beads, the bolts of cloth, the pretty brass dishes— But, *haba!* They are just going in to sing to the patients in the hospital there. It isn't even market day. There won't be any crowds or any nice things to see. There's a big government hospital in Market Town. Lots of sick folks are there. Father says we can go in and sing to them. He says they'll like it. Well, maybe, but I don't see why I have to go.

Baba tossed me a peanut that was still warm from roasting. I cracked the shell.

"We've had a good peanut crop this year," Baba said. "Lots of good things have happened to us this year."

"We've had lots of peanuts," I agreed as I reached for another one. "Little Lion and I each received a whole pound for our crop," I reminded Grandfather. A whole pound! That's a lot of money. I'd bought a new *zane* to wear, a nice bright red cloth with yellow stripes in it.

And I'd bought a pair of red goatskin sandals.
And I even had seven shillings left! I really felt
rich. Yes, the Lord Jesus had really been good
to us. I had a good home, lots of money—

"The Lord's been good to us this year," Baba
said. It was almost like he was reading my mind.
"We ought to be awfully grateful."

"We surely ought to," I answered as I plopped
a handful of peanuts into my mouth.

Baba reached for another nut. "I heard you
talking to your father about going to the hospital to sing."

"Oh, Baba! I don't see why I have to go."

"You don't have to go." Baba smiled.

I ate another peanut. It didn't taste so good.

Baba poked at the fire with his long walking
stick.

"Want to hear a story before you crawl onto
your sleeping mat?" he asked.

"Oh, yes, please!" Baba's stories are always so
good. I pulled my blanket up around my shoulders and tossed a piece of wood on the fire. The
red and orange sparks shot up into the black
sky. Somewhere, out in the distance, a hyena
howled.

"Once upon a time, in the city of Kano, there

lived a very wealthy chief. Now, this chief was very, very rich, and very, very good. Every morning he would get on his fine white horse and ride around the town and greet all his loyal subjects. If he would see anyone who was in need, he would give him a gift of money.

"There was one beggar who sat by the gate of the city every day and begged. Every day the chief would come by and toss the beggar a gift. The beggar would bow low and say, 'Oh, Chief, long life to you, sir. You are so good to me. All I have comes from you. Without your help this poor old beggar would starve to death.'

"The good chief would smile at him and go about his business of helping people. The next day the old beggar would be waiting beside the gate; and when the chief would come by, the old beggar would bow low and scrape his nose in the dust and say, 'Oh, sir, you are so kind. I thank you for this gift. I do appreciate your help. Thank you very much.'

"The next morning the faithful chief would go about the town passing out his good gifts and helping those in need. He would come to the old beggar and give him some money or grain or, once in a while, even a robe.

The beggar went to the city every day and begged.

"The old beggar would fall to the ground and whine, 'I am your faithful slave. I couldn't live without you. I appreciate your help. You are so kind. Thank you, sir, thank you!'

"This went on for years. Never once did the chief fail to give the old beggar a good gift. One morning the chief started out on his rounds of helping the people. When he got to the old beggar, he gave him his gift and then said, 'Beggar, I have a very important meeting I must go to. I forgot to tell my servants to water my favorite horse. I wonder if you would go to the palace and give my horse some water. I'd appreciate it very much. He might suffer greatly in the heat if he does not have his water today.'

"Quickly the old beggar stood up. He shook the dust off his robes and sneered, 'Sir, I'll take your gifts, but I won't run your errands!'"

I got up. "Baba, I think I've got to go to bed now. I have an errand to do in the morning. I want to get up early and go with Mother and Father to Market Town to sing in the hospital."

8

Elder Turtle and the Robe

I was sure no one had seen me. It was just lying there—the penny, I mean—right on the floor by Mari's desk at school. It wasn't like I'd taken it off her desk. That would be stealing.

But, well, I don't know. I felt the penny in my pocket, and it seemed like it was burning right into my leg. It felt awfully heavy. And, I didn't feel so good. But, after all, I don't know for sure it was Mari's penny. I did see her looking for something though.

Oh, there's no use in trying to fool myself. I did know that it was her penny! But, no one would ever find out. I was sure of that.

I pulled the penny out of my pocket. That would buy another bead for my necklace. I would look so pretty in that necklace. I sighed.

Somehow—well, I don't know. I didn't feel so good about that necklace now.

"You sighed. What's the matter, Sunday? When you set aside your heart like that, I know there's something wrong." Baba sat down beside me.

"Oh, nothing," I answered.

"Are you sure?" he questioned.

"Nothing's wrong!" I felt real cross. I looked down at the penny in my hand.

"What's that you've got?" Baba asked.

"A penny."

Just then, Little Lion came running into the compound. He plopped himself down on the mat beside me.

"You know what?" he asked. He sounded excited.

"What?" Baba smiled.

It's a good thing somebody feels like smiling around here, I thought.

"I just saw Mari and she said she's lost a penny."

Quickly I put the penny into my pocket. Why, oh, why, did this have to happen to me?

"And," Little Lion went on as he looked at me, "she's mad. She says that Sunday went by her desk and she stole that penny. And she says if that's the kind of a girl Christians are—well, she doesn't want to be one."

Baba looked at me. I felt my face burning.

"Isn't Mari the girl you've been trying to get to come to Sunday school?" Baba asked.

"Yes," I answered. "Baba, I just found the penny."

"But, it was on Mari's desk, wasn't it?" Baba asked softly.

"No, it was on the floor by her desk."

"And didn't you think it might be hers?" Baba said softly.

"Yes." I hung my head.

"Let me tell you a story, Sunday," Baba said.

I didn't want to hear a story. I felt awful.

But Baba didn't wait to find out if I wanted to hear a story or not. He just began talking.

"One time there was a turtle—a big old turtle. Now, this turtle was one of the leading elders in his village. Oh, he was a fine big turtle. Everyone liked Elder Turtle and bowed to him when he went strolling down the paths of their village.

"Elder Turtle's shell was fine and hard, and he kept it polished with peanut oil. Oh, he just sparkled when he walked through the town.

"And everyone respected him. All the mothers of the little mice and weasels and frogs would say, 'If you only grow up to be as fine and as honest and as good as Elder Turtle is, then I'll be happy.'

"Yes, everyone liked Elder Turtle and looked up to him. Of course Elder Turtle enjoyed all this praise. Every time he'd hear someone say how good he was, it just seemed that his shell would grow another quarter of an inch.

"And then, too, he always had a good word of advice for the other turtles and squirrels and birds in his village. 'You should be like I am,' he would tell them. And of course everyone would agree that Elder Turtle's advice was right.

"One bright sunny day Elder Turtle heard the town crier. Quickly Elder Turtle crawled out of his hole under the kapok tree and lumbered off to the marketplace to hear the news.

Squeaky squirrel was pounding on his drum and shouting out the big news: 'Big political meeting! Big political meeting! Come to the market tomorrow and vote for a new chief!'

"Elder Turtle listened carefully and then headed for home. He was very interested in politics. Elder Turtle wanted to be elected chief of the town. There was nothing that Elder Turtle wanted more than being chief.

" 'Think how wonderful it would be to have folks bow before me and say, "Long life to you, Chief!" ' Elder Turtle said to himself. He sighed. Oh, that would be wonderful to have everyone respect him, to look up to him, to bow when he came into a group. How wonderful!

" 'And think of all the good that I can do,' he told himself. 'I'll make everyone mind me. They'll do just as I say, and we'll have a wonderful village. Oh, yes, it will be just marvelous to be chief. I do so want to be chief. And I'll be a good chief.'

"As he walked along toward his house, Elder Turtle made all sorts of plans about what he would do when he was elected chief. Now Squeaky Squirrel's house lay between Elder Turtle's hole and the marketplace. So when Elder Turtle came alongside Squeaky Squirrel's house, he happened to see a lovely new robe hanging on the line. Elder Turtle stopped to admire it.

" 'That is a lovely robe,' he said to himself. 'I'll bet it cost a lot of money.' He turned and started away. Then he stopped. 'If I had that robe, I could sell it and buy myself a nice new turban. I'd surely look good in a turban when I'm elected chief of the village.' Again he started away, and then turned back. 'Yes, sir,' he said, 'if I had that robe I could buy a really good turban. Not just a cheap old thing. Everyone would say, "Doesn't our chief look beautiful in his new turban?" '

"Elder Turtle sighed and started home. Suddenly he stopped. He had a wonderful plan. Elder Turtle went home and waited impatiently for night to come. 'No one will ever know,' he told himself. Late that night, when it was very dark, Elder Turtle crawled out of his hole and hurried down to Squeaky Squirrel's house. Quietly he put his right hand through the window to feel for the robe.

" 'I'm sure Squeaky Squirrel will never miss it! And besides, he'll never know where it went.' His right hand felt around inside the window. Yes, there was the fine robe lying on a chair directly beneath the window. Quietly, very quietly, he began to pull it toward him. As he drew the robe gently, suddenly it caught on something. He gave a tug, and there was a crash!

"Squeaky Squirrel jumped out of bed and raced to the window. He saw a hand tugging at his robe. Quickly he grabbed a sharp knife and, with one quick blow, chopped off Elder Turtle's right hand.

"Elder Turtle drew back into the darkness. He limped off toward his hole as fast as he could. He tried to comfort himself. 'I'm lucky. No one need ever know.'

"The next morning Elder Turtle hobbled off to the political meeting. He wasn't very happy, but he tried to cheer himself up by reminding himself that surely no one would ever find out what had happened.

"The meeting had just begun when Elder Turtle arrived. Squeaky Squirrel was the chairman.

" 'Now,' said Squeaky Squirrel, 'we will have the voting for a new chief. The vote will be for either Elder Turtle or Messenger Mouse. Now, all in favor of Messenger Mouse being elected, raise his right hand.'

"Squeaky Squirrel counted the right hands, 'Twenty-two, twenty-three, twenty-four. Twenty-four votes for Messenger Mouse!'

"Elder Turtle's heart was pounding. Oh, he

wanted to be elected chief so very much. It was his dearest wish.

" 'Now,' said Squeaky Squirrel, 'we will vote on Elder Turtle. Everyone in favor of Elder Turtle being chief, raise his right hand.'

"Elder Turtle was so excited about the voting that he forgot his right hand was cut off. He raised his right arm, but there was no hand on it. Squeaky Squirrel started counting, 'Twenty-two, twenty-three—'And then he looked at Elder Turtle.

"No right hand!

"Squeaky Squirrel's eyebrows shot up. Elder Turtle looked at Squeaky Squirrel and wondered at the strange expression on his face. And then—suddenly—he realized. Quickly he pulled his stump down and hid it under his shell.

"Squeaky Squirrel said, 'Well, it seems that Elder Turtle has lost his voting hand. So that's twenty-three votes for Elder Turtle. Messenger Mouse wins the election!'

"Elder Turtle knew that Squeaky Squirrel had found out about him.

" 'Now Squeaky Squirrel and the others in the town will never listen to me or respect me,' Elder Turtle cried to himself. He was so

Elder turtle forgot his hand was cut off.

ashamed that he sneaked off and hid in his hole and never came out again."

"Baba,"I said as I pulled the penny out of my pocket, "I've got some voting to do. I've got to see Mari. I'll be back soon."

9

The Burden of Black Beans

"Baba," I begged, "tell us a story."

The fire was burning low. The sky was dark. It was very quiet except for the faraway beating of drums across the town. It was nice there by the fire, but a little sad, and a little lonely.

Baba laid the little *faifai* he was weaving down on the lion-skin mat. I rubbed the old mat. We'd heard lots of wonderful stories while we were on this old mat. Baba smiled at me. Baba is awfully nice. I think he's the nicest grandfather in the whole wide world.

"Oh, yes, Baba, do tell us a story," Little Lion coaxed.

Baba tossed a stick of wood on the fire. The orangy sparks flew upward and died in the cold black sky. I shivered a little bit and moved over closer to Baba.

"I've been thinking about a true story," Baba said as he tugged at his scrawny gray beard.

"Oh, Baba, true stories are the very best," I said.

"This is a true story that happened when our country was very young. Every father for many generations has been telling his son this story. It is the best-loved story of our people."

"Tell it to me so that I will be able to tell my son," Little Lion laughed.

"It is very sad," Baba cautioned.

"Tell it to us, please," we said.

"Once upon a time, 'way up in the far north, when our country was very young, there was a wicked king. He was a very lazy, mean old king who loved no one but himself and his only son, Dan Mugu. When Dan Mugu was a very little boy, the old king sent a messenger out into the village to look for a little child the same age and size of Dan Mugu. They searched many houses, and finally, in the house of the gourd-mender, they found a young boy named Black Beans. This young child was chosen to be the whipping boy of Dan Mugu."

I shuddered. "Oh, the poor boy. I wouldn't want to be anyone's whipping boy. You mean, every time the chief's son, Dan Mugu, was bad, you mean—poor Black Beans was whipped?"

"Yes, Sunday, the son of the wicked king was never punished. If Dan Mugu did something naughty, then Black Beans was called in and he took the punishment for Dan Mugu."

"Wish I had a whipping boy," Little Lion muttered.

"And so, of course, Dan Mugu grew into a wicked, proud young man who never thought of anyone's feelings but his own. When he was eighteen, Dan Mugu was considered too old to be punished, so his whipping boy, Black Beans, was allowed to go back to his home in the village.

"Everyone loved Black Beans as much as they hated Dan Mugu. If Black Beans saw anyone in trouble, he was the first to help. If someone needed a hand with his farming, or in building a new house, or in putting on a new roof, it was Black Beans who was right there to offer help.

"With Dan Mugu, it was just the opposite. Folks ran and hid when they saw him coming. Dan Mugu would ride his fine black horse through the streets of the village. And if anyone got in his way—man or woman or child—he would ride right over him. If Dan Mugu saw something he wanted, he demanded that thing and got it. No one dared refuse him because he was the son of the powerful king.

"One day Black Beans was coming in from his farm when he heard the dreaded fire call, '*EEEow! EEEEEow!*' Throwing his hoe over his shoulder, he raced into the village to help fight the fire. The marketplace was ablaze.

" 'What—what happened?' Black Beans gasped as he raced for a bucket of water.

" 'Dan Mugu!' one of the townsmen spit in disgust. 'Dan Mugu did it.'

" 'What did he do?' Black Beans cried. 'How could he cause all this damage?'

" 'Dan Mugu didn't like the meat that Ali, the meat seller, gave him. And so, Dan Mugu scattered the burning coals of Ali's fire with his riding whip. And now, look! Look at our market!'

"Black Beans raised his eyes and looked across the marketplace: blackened walls, where once happy traders had bartered for corn and cloth. His eyes swept over the ruins. The tree under which his father had sat mending broken gourds and fashioning designs on new ones, still

The villagers ran to escape the burning marketplace.

smoked. And the burned remains of many days' labor lay smoking at its base.

"Here and there he could see sweat-streaked, soot-covered people scraping around in the ashes trying to rescue some bit or piece that could be sold.

"Sadly, Black Beans turned away. It was so useless, this waste. It was so wicked. The whole market destroyed because of the evilness of the chief's son! Black Beans sighed. Would no one ever remove this burden, Dan Mugu, from the people?

"Black Beans started for his home to find out if he was needed there. He walked with dragging feet and a dark stomach. He was so unhappy and grieved at the sorrow that Dan Mugu had caused.

"Black Beans followed the twisting, narrow path to his house. Suddenly, he heard new screams, '*EEEow! EEEEow!* Our house is on fire.'

"More wickedness from the king's son? Black Beans raced to help the struggling family rescue their few belongings from the flaming house. But before he reached the house, a voice called out, 'Black Beans! Black Beans! *Stop!'*

"Black Beans halted in his tracks. He saw the chief's son, Dan Mugu. *Now what evil would he be doing?* Black Beans thought.

" 'Black Beans, come here!' the wicked Dan Mugu screamed. 'My horse has gone lame, and I must have a horse to ride. You—you my friend —you, my whipping boy—*you* shall be my horse!'

"And with these words Dan Mugu gave a mighty leap and jumped onto the shoulders of Black Beans!

" '*Yi!* Now run, you beast!' Dan Mugu laughed and struck Black Beans about the head with his whip. 'Run! You're my horse!'

"Suddenly a gleam came into Black Beans' eyes. 'I'll run!' he cried. 'And you'll run with me—*to your death!'*

"And Black Beans plunged into the flaming house. Dan Mugu gave a horrible scream, and then there was silence. Black Beans had rid the town of the burden of their enemy, Dan Mugu. But, he had given his life to do it."

I rubbed the lion-skin mat. It felt soft and comfortable to my touch. The night was quiet; even the drums had stopped.

"Baba," I said, "there was Somebody else who

Black Beans plunged into the flaming house.

did that so we could be free from wickedness. The Lord Jesus Christ gave His life so that we could be free from the burden of sin."